FARMER GILES
OF HAM

By J. R. R. Tolkien

The Hobbit
The Lord of the Rings
The Fellowship of the Ring
The Two Towers
The Return of the King
The Silmarillion
The Adventures of Tom Bombadil
Tree and Leaf
Smith of Wootton Major
Sir Gawain and the Green Knight, Pearl
and Sir Orfeo
Mr. Bliss
The Father Christmas Letters
Unfinished Tales
and, edited by Christopher Tolkien,
The History of Middle-earth
The Book of Lost Tales
The Lays of Beleriand
The Shaping of Middle-earth
The Lost Road
The Return of the Shadow
The Treason of Isengard
The War of the Ring

J. R. R. TOLKIEN

FARMER GILES OF HAM

Aegidii Ahenobarbi Julii Agricole de Hammo
Domini de Domito
Aule Draconarie Comitis
Regni Minimi Regis et Basilei
mira facinora et mirabilis exortus

or in the vulgar tongue

The Rise and Wonderful Adventures
of Farmer Giles, Lord of Tame
Count of Worminghall and
King of the Little Kingdom

With illustrations by Roger Garland

UNWIN
PAPERBACKS

LONDON SYDNEY WELLINGTON

First published in 1949
Second impression 1957
Third impression 1961
Fourth impression 1965
Fifth impression 1966
Sixth impression 1969
Seventh impression 1970
Eighth impression 1971
Ninth impression 1972
Tenth impression 1973
Eleventh impression 1974
Reset New Format 1976
Reset New Format 1990

This new reset format first published in Great Britain by
Unwin Hyman, an imprint of Unwin Hyman Limited, 1990

UNWIN HYMAN LIMITED
15–17 Broadwick Street, London W1V 1FP

Allen & Unwin Australia Pty Ltd,
8 Napier Street, North Sydney, NSW 2060, Australia

Allen & Unwin with the Port Nicholson Press
Compusales Building, 75 Ghuznee Street, Wellington, New Zealand

A CIP catalogue record for this book is available
from the British Library.

Paperback ISBN 0–04–440723–8
Hardback ISBN 0–04–440724–6

Set in 11½ on 13 point Bembo by
Nene Phototypesetters Ltd, Northampton
and printed in Great Britain by
Cox and Wyman Ltd, Reading

To C. H. Wilkinson

Foreword

Of the history of the Little Kingdom few frag-
ments have survived; but by chance an account of
its origin has been preserved: a legend, perhaps,
rather than an account; for it is evidently a late
compilation, full of marvels, derived not from
sober annals, but from the popular lays to which
its author frequently refers. For him the events
that he records lay already in a distant past; but he
seems, nonetheless, to have lived himself in the
lands of the Little Kingdom. Such geographical
knowledge as he shows (it is not his strong point)
is of that country, while of regions outside it,
north or west, he is plainly ignorant.

An excuse for presenting a translation of this
curious tale, out of its very insular Latin into the
modern tongue of the United Kingdom, may be
found in the glimpse that it affords of life in a dark
period of the history of Britain, not to mention
the light that it throws on the origin of some
difficult place-names. Some may find the charac-
ter and adventures of its hero attractive in themselves.

The boundaries of the Little Kingdom, either in
time or space, are not easy to determine from the
scanty evidence. Since Brutus came to Britain
many kings and realms have come and gone. The
partition under Locrin, Camber, and Albanac,
was only the first of many shifting divisions.
What with the love of petty independence on the
one hand, and on the other the greed of kings for

wider realms, the years were filled with swift alternations of war and peace, of mirth and woe, as historians of the reign of Arthur tell us: a time of unsettled frontiers, when men might rise or fall suddenly, and song-writers had abundant material and eager audiences. Somewhere in those long years, after the days of King Coel maybe, but before Arthur or the Seven Kingdoms of the English, we must place the events here related; and their scene is the valley of the Thames, with an excursion north-west to the walls of Wales.

The capital of the Little Kingdom was evidently, as is ours, in its south-east corner, but its confines are vague. It seems never to have reached far up the Thames into the West, nor beyond Otmoor to the North; its eastern borders are dubious. There are indications in a fragmentary legend of Georgius son of Giles and his page Suovetaurilius (Suet) that at one time an outpost against the Middle Kingdom was maintained at Farthingho. But that situation does not concern this story, which is now presented without alteration or further comment, though the original grandiose title has been suitably reduced to *Farmer Giles of Ham*.

Farmer Giles
of Ham

Ægidius de Hammo was a man who lived in the midmost parts of the Island of Britain. In full his name was Ægidius Ahenobarbus Julius Agricola de Hammo; for people were richly endowed with names in those days, now long ago, when this island was still happily divided into many kingdoms. There was more time then, and folk were fewer, so that most men were distinguished. However, those days are now over, so I will in what follows give the man his name shortly, and in the vulgar form: he was Farmer Giles of Ham, and he had a red beard. Ham was only a village, but villages were proud and independent still in those days.

Farmer Giles had a dog. The dog's name was Garm. Dogs had to be content with short names in the vernacular: the Book-latin was reserved for their betters. Garm could not talk even dog-latin; but he could use the vulgar tongue (as could most

1

dogs of his day) either to bully or to brag or to wheedle in. Bullying was for beggars and trespassers, bragging for other dogs, and wheedling for his master. Garm was both proud and afraid of Giles, who could bully and brag better than he could.

The time was not one of hurry or bustle. But bustle has very little to do with business. Men did their work without it; and they got through a deal both of work and of talk. There was plenty to talk about, for memorable events occurred very frequently. But at the moment when this tale begins nothing memorable had, in fact, happened in Ham for quite a long time. Which suited Farmer Giles down to the ground: he was a slow sort of fellow, rather set in his ways, and taken up with his own affairs. He had his hands full (he said) keeping the wolf from the door: that is, keeping himself as fat and comfortable as his father before him. The dog was busy helping him. Neither of them gave much thought to the Wide World outside their fields, the village, and the nearest market.

But the Wide World was there. The forest was not far off, and away west and north were the Wild Hills, and the dubious marches of the mountain-country. And among other things still at large there were giants: rude and uncultured folk, and troublesome at times. There was one giant in particular, larger and more stupid than his fellows. I find no mention of his name in the histories, but it does not matter. He was very large, his walking-stick was like a tree, and his tread was heavy. He brushed elms aside like tall grasses; and he was the ruin of roads and the desolation of gardens, for his great feet made holes in them as deep as wells; if he stumbled into a house, that was the end of it. And all this damage he did wherever he went, for his head was far above the roofs of houses and left his feet to look after themselves. He was near-sighted and also rather deaf. Fortunately he lived far off in the Wild, and seldom visited the lands inhabited by men, at least not on purpose. He had a great tumbledown house away up in the mountains; but he had very few friends, owing to his deafness and his stupidity, and the scarcity of giants. He used to go out walking in the Wild Hills and in the empty regions at the feet of the mountains, all by himself.

One fine summer's day this giant went out for a walk, and wandered aimlessly along, doing a great deal of damage in the woods. Suddenly he noticed that the sun was setting, and felt that his supper-time was drawing near; but he discovered that he was in a part of the country that he did not know at all and had lost his way. Making a wrong guess at the right direction he walked and he walked until it was dark night. Then he sat down and waited for the moon to rise. Then he walked and walked in the moonlight, striding out with a will, for he was anxious to get home. He had left his best copper pot on the fire, and feared that the bottom would be burned. But his back was to the

mountains, and he was already in the lands inhabited by men. He was, indeed, now drawing
near to the farm of Ægidius Ahenobarbus Julius
Agricola and the village called (in the vulgar
tongue) Ham.

It was a fine night. The cows were in the fields,
and Farmer Giles's dog had got out and gone for
a walk on his own account. He had a fancy
for moonshine, and rabbits. He had no idea, of
course, that a giant was also out for a walk. That
would have given him a good reason for going
out without leave, but a still better reason for
staying quiet in the kitchen. At about two o'clock
the giant arrived in Farmer Giles's fields, broke
the hedges, trampled on the crops, and flattened
the mowing-grass. In five minutes he had done
more damage than the royal fox-hunt could have
done in five days.

Garm heard a thump-thump coming along the
riverbank, and he ran to the west side of the low
hill on which the farmhouse stood, just to see
what was happening. Suddenly he saw the giant
stride right across the river and tread upon
Galathea, the farmer's favourite cow, squashing

4

the poor beast as flat as the farmer could have squashed a blackbeetle.

That was more than enough for Garm. He gave a yelp of fright and bolted home. Quite forgetting that he was out without leave, he came and barked and yammered underneath his master's bedroom window. There was no answer for a long time. Farmer Giles was not easily wakened.

'Help! help! help!' cried Garm.

The window opened suddenly and a well-aimed bottle came flying out.

'Ow!' said the dog, jumping aside with practised skill. 'Help! help! help!'

Out popped the farmer's head. 'Drat you, dog! What be you a-doing?' said he.

'Nothing,' said the dog.

'I'll give you nothing! I'll flay the skin off you in the morning,' said the farmer, slamming the window.

'Help! help! help!' cried the dog.

Out came Giles's head again. 'I'll kill you, if you make another sound,' he said. 'What's come to you, you fool?'

'Nothing,' said the dog; 'but something's come to you.'

'What d'you mean?' said Giles, startled in the midst of his rage. Never before had Garm answered him saucily.

'There's a giant in your fields, an enormous giant; and he's coming this way,' said the dog. 'Help! help! He is trampling on your sheep. He has stamped on poor Galathea, and she's as flat as

a doormat. Help! help! He's bursting all your hedges, and he's crushing all your crops. You must be bold and quick, master, or you will soon have nothing left. Help!' Garm began to howl.

'Shut up!' said the farmer, and he shut the window. 'Lord-a-mercy!' he said to himself; and though the night was warm, he shivered and shook.

'Get back to bed and don't be a fool!' said his wife. 'And drown that dog in the morning. There is no call to believe what a dog says; they'll tell any tale, when caught truant or thieving.'

'May be, Agatha,' said he, 'and may be not. But there's something going on in my fields, or Garm's a rabbit. That dog was frightened. And why should he come yammering in the night when he could sneak in at the back door with the milk in the morning?'

'Don't stand there arguing!' said she. 'If you believe the dog, then take his advice: be bold and quick!'

'Easier said than done,' answered Giles; for, indeed, he believed quite half of Garm's tale. In the small hours of the night giants seem less unlikely.

Still, property is property; and Farmer Giles had a short way with trespassers that few could outface. So he pulled on his breeches, and went down into the kitchen and took his blunderbuss from the wall. Some may well ask what a blunderbuss was. Indeed, this very question, it is said.

7

was put to the Four Wise Clerks of Oxenford, and after thought they replied: 'A blunderbuss is a short gun with a large bore firing many balls or slugs, and capable of doing execution within a limited range without exact aim. (Now superseded in civilised countries by other firearms.)'

However, Farmer Giles's blunderbuss had a wide mouth that opened like a horn, and it did not fire balls or slugs, but anything that he could spare to stuff in. And it did not do execution, because he seldom loaded it, and never let it off. The sight of it was usually enough for his purpose. And this country was not yet civilized, for the blunderbuss was not superseded: it was indeed the only kind of gun that there was, and rare at that. People

8

preferred bows and arrows and used gunpower mostly for fireworks.

Well then, Farmer Giles took down the blunderbuss, and he put in a good charge of powder, just in case extreme measures should be required; and into the wide mouth he stuffed old nails and bits of wire, pieces of broken pot, bones and stones and other rubbish. Then he drew on his top-boots and his overcoat, and he went out through the kitchen garden.

The moon was low behind him, and he could see nothing worse than the long black shadows of bushes and trees; but he could hear a dreadful stamping-stumping coming up the side of the hill. He did not feel either bold or quick, whatever Agatha might say; but he was more anxious about his property than his skin. So, feeling a bit loose about the belt, he walked towards the brow of the hill.

Suddenly up over the edge of it the giant's face appeared, pale in the moonlight, which glittered in his large round eyes. His feet were still far below, making holes in the fields. The moon dazzled the giant and he did not see the farmer; but Farmer Giles saw him and was scared out of his wits. He pulled the trigger without thinking, and the blunderbuss went off with a staggering bang. By luck it was pointed more or less at the giant's large ugly face. Out flew the rubbish, and the stones and the bones, and the bits of crock and wire, and half a dozen nails. And since the range was indeed limited, by chance and no choice of

the farmer's many of these things struck the giant: a piece of pot went in his eye, and a large nail stuck in his nose.

'Blast!' said the giant in his vulgar fashion. 'I'm stung!' The noise had made no impression on him (he was rather deaf), but he did not like the nail. It was a long time since he had met any insect fierce enough to pierce his thick skin; but he had heard tell that away East, in the Fens, there were dragonflies that could bite like hot pincers. He thought that he must have run into something of the kind.

'Nasty unhealthy parts, evidently,' said he. 'I shan't go any further this way tonight.'

So he picked up a couple of sheep off the hill-side, to eat when he got home, and went back over the river, making off about nor-nor-west at a great pace. He found his way home again in the end, for he was at last going in the right direction; but the bottom was burned off his copper pot.

As for Farmer Giles, when the blunderbuss went off it knocked him over flat on his back; and there he lay looking at the sky and wondering if the giant's feet would miss him as they passed by. But nothing happened, and the stamping-stumping died away in the distance. So he got up, rubbed his shoulder, and picked up the blunder-buss. Then suddenly he heard the sound of people cheering.

Most of the people of Ham had been looking out of their windows; a few had put on their clothes and come out (after the giant had gone

11

away). Some were now running up the hill shouting.

The villagers had heard the horrible thump-thump of the giant's feet, and most of them had immediately got under the bed-clothes; some had got under the beds. But Garm was both proud and frightened of his master. He thought him terrible and splendid, when he was angry; and he naturally thought that any giant would think the same. So, as soon as he saw Giles come out with the blunderbuss (a sign of great wrath as a rule), he rushed off to the village, barking and crying:

'Come out! Come out! Come out! Get up! Get up! Come and see my great master! He is bold and quick. He is going to shoot a giant for trespassing. Come out!'

The top of the hill could be seen from most of the houses. When the people and the dog saw the giant's face rise above it, they quailed and held their breath, and all but the dog among them thought that this would prove a matter too big for Giles to deal with. Then the blunderbuss went bang, and the giant turned suddenly and went away, and in their amazement and their joy they clapped and cheered, and Garm nearly barked his head off.

'Hooray!' they shouted. 'That will learn him! Master Ægidius has given him what for. Now he will go home and die, and serve him right and proper.' Then they all cheered again together. But even as they cheered, they took note for their own profit that after all this blunderbuss could really be fired. There had been some debate in the village inns on that point; but now the matter was settled. Farmer Giles had little trouble with trespassers after that.

When all seemed safe some of the bolder folk came right up the hill and shook hands with Farmer Giles. A few – the parson, and the blacksmith, and the miller, and one or two other persons of importance – slapped him on the back. That did not please him (his shoulder was very sore), but he felt obliged to invite them into his house. They sat round in the kitchen drinking his health and loudly praising him. He made no effort to hide his yawns, but as long as the drink lasted they took no notice. By the time they had all had one or two (and the farmer two or three), he began to feel quite bold; when they had all had two or three (and he himself five or six), he felt as bold as his dog thought him. They parted good friends; and he slapped their backs heartily. His hands were large, red, and thick; so he had his revenge.

Next day he found that the news had grown in the telling, and he had become an important local figure. By the middle of the next week the news had spread to all the villages within twenty miles. He had become the Hero of the Countryside. Very pleasant he found it. Next market day he got enough free drink to float a boat: that is to say, he nearly had his fill, and came home singing old heroic songs.

At last even the Kings got to hear of it. The capital of that realm, the Middle Kingdom of the island in those happy days, was some twenty leagues distant from Ham, and they paid little heed at court, as a rule, to the doings of rustics in the provinces. But so prompt an expulsion of a giant so injurious seemed worthy of note and of some little courtesy. So in due course – that is, about three months, and on the feast of St Michael – the King sent a magnificent letter. It was written in red upon white parchment, and expressed the royal approbation of 'our loyal subject and well-beloved Ægidius Ahenobarbus Julius Agricola de Hammo'.

The letter was signed with a red blot; but the court scribe had added: 𝕰𝖌𝖔 𝕬𝖚𝖌𝖚𝖘𝖙𝖚𝖘 𝕭𝖔𝖓𝖎𝖋𝖆𝖈𝖎𝖚𝖘 𝕬𝖒𝖇𝖗𝖔𝖘𝖎𝖚𝖘 𝕬𝖚𝖗𝖊𝖑𝖎𝖆𝖓𝖚𝖘 𝕬𝖓𝖙𝖔𝖓𝖎𝖓𝖚𝖘 𝕻𝖎𝖚𝖘 𝖊𝖙 𝕸𝖆𝖌𝖓𝖎𝖋𝖎𝖈𝖚𝖘, 𝖉𝖚𝖝 𝖗𝖊𝖝, 𝖙𝖞𝖗𝖆𝖓𝖓𝖚𝖘, 𝖊𝖙 𝕭𝖆𝖘𝖎𝖑𝖊𝖚𝖘 𝕸𝖊𝖉𝖎𝖙𝖊𝖗𝖗𝖆𝖓𝖊𝖆𝖗𝖚𝖒 𝕻𝖆𝖗𝖙𝖎𝖚𝖒, 𝖘𝖚𝖇𝖘𝖈𝖗𝖎𝖇𝖔; and a large red seal was attached. So the document was plainly genuine. It afforded great pleasure to Giles, and was much admired, especially when it was discovered that one could get a seat and a drink by the farmer's fire by asking to look at it.

Better than the testimonial was the accompanying gift. The King sent a belt and a long sword. To tell the truth the King had never used the

sword himself. It belonged to the family and had been hanging in his armoury time out of mind. The armourer could not say how it came there, or what might be the use of it. Plain heavy swords of that kind were out of fashion at court just then, so the King thought it the very thing for a present to a rustic. But Farmer Giles was delighted, and his local reputation became enormous.

Giles much enjoyed the turn of events. So did his dog. He never got his promised whipping. Giles was a just man according to his lights; in his heart he gave a fair share of the credit to Garm, though he never went so far as to mention it. He continued to throw hard words and hard things at the dog when he felt inclined, but he winked at many little outings. Garm took to walking far afield. The farmer went about with a high step, and luck smiled on him. The autumn and early winter work went well. All seemed set fair – until the dragon came.

In those days dragons were already getting scarce in the island. None had been seen in the midland realm of Augustus Bonifacius for many a year. There were, of course, the dubious marches and the uninhabited mountains, westward and northward, but they were a long way off. In those parts once upon a time there had dwelt a number of dragons of one kind and another, and they had made raids far and wide. But the Middle Kingdom was in those days famous for the daring of the King's knights, and so many stray dragons had been killed, or had returned with grave

16

damage, that the others gave up going that way.

It was still the custom for Dragon's Tail to be served up at the King's Christmas Feast; and each year a knight was chosen for the duty of hunting. He was supposed to set out upon St Nicholas' Day and come home with a dragon's tail not later than the eve of the feast. But for many years now the Royal Cook had made a marvellous confection, a Mock Dragon's Tail of cake and almond-paste, with cunning scales of hard icing-sugar. The chosen knight then carried this into the hall on Christmas Eve, while the fiddles played and the trumpets rang. The Mock Dragon's Tail was eaten after dinner on Christmas Day, and everybody said (to please the cook) that it tasted much better than Real Tail.

That was the situation when a real dragon turned up again. The giant was largely to blame. After his adventure he used to go about in the mountains visiting his scattered relations more than had been his custom, and much more than they liked. For he was always trying to borrow a large copper pot. But whether he got the loan of one or not, he would sit and talk in his long-winded lumbering fashion about the excellent country down away East, and all the wonders of the Wide World. He had got it into his head that he was a great and daring traveller.

'A nice land,' he would say, 'pretty flat, soft to the feet, and plenty to eat for the taking: cows, you know, and sheep all over the place, easy to spot, if you look carefully.'

'But what about the people?' said they.

'I never saw any,' said he. 'There was not a knight to be seen or heard, my dear fellows. Nothing worse than a few stinging flies by the river.'

'Why don't you go back and stay there?' said they.

'Oh well, there's no place like home, they say,' said he. 'But maybe I shall go back one day when I have a mind. And anyway I went there once, which is more than most folk can say. Now about that copper pot.'

'And these rich lands,' they would hurriedly ask, 'these delectable regions full of undefended cattle, which way do they lie? And how far off?'

'Oh,' he would answer, 'away east or sou'east. But it's a long journey.' And then he would give such an exaggerated account of the distance that he had walked, and the woods, hills, and plains that he had crossed, that none of the other less long-legged giants ever set out. Still, the talk got about.

Then the warm summer was followed by a hard winter. It was bitter cold in the mountains and food was scarce. The talk got louder. Lowland sheep and kine from the deep pastures were much discussed. The dragons pricked up their ears. They were hungry, and these rumours were attractive.

'So knights are mythical!' said the younger and less experienced dragons. 'We always thought so.'

'At least they may be getting rare,' thought the

older and wiser worms; 'far and few and no longer to be feared.'

There was one dragon who was deeply moved. Chrysophylax Dives was his name, for he was of ancient and imperial lineage, and very rich. He was cunning, inquisitive, greedy, well-armoured, but not over bold. But at any rate he was not in the least afraid of flies or insects of any sort or size; and he was mortally hungry.

So one winter's day, about a week before Christmas, Chrysophylax spread his wings and took off. He landed quietly in the middle of the night plump in the heart of the midland realm of Augustus Bonifacius rex et basileus. He did a deal of damage in a short while, smashing and burning, and devouring sheep, cattle, and horses.

This was in a part of the land a long way from Ham, but Garm got the fright of his life. He had gone off on a long expedition, and taking advantage of his master's favour he had ventured to spend a night or two away from home. He was following an engaging scent along the eaves of a wood, when he turned a corner and came suddenly upon a new and alarming smell; he ran indeed slap into the tail of Chrysophylax Dives, who had just landed. Never did a dog turn his own tail round and bolt home swifter than Garm. The dragon, hearing his yelp, turned and snorted; but Garm was already far out of range. He ran all the rest of the night, and arrived home about breakfast-time.

'Help! help! help!' he cried outside the back door.

Giles heard, and did not like the sound of it. It reminded him that unexpected things may happen, when all seems to be going well.

'Wife, let that dratted dog in,' said he, 'and take a stick to him!'

Garm came bundling into the kitchen with his eyes starting and his tongue hanging out. 'Help!' he cried.

'Now what have you been a–doing this time?' said Giles, throwing a sausage at him.

'Nothing,' panted Garm, too flustered to give heed to the sausage.

'Well, stop doing it, or I'll skin you,' said the farmer.

'I've done no wrong. I didn't mean no harm,' said the dog. 'But I came on a dragon accidental-like, and it frightened me.'

The farmer choked in his beer. 'Dragon?' said he. 'Drat you for a good-for-nothing nosey-parker! What d'you want to go and find a dragon for, at this time of the year, and me with my hands full? Where was it?'

'Oh! North over the hills and far away, beyond the Standing Stones and all,' said the dog.

'Oh, away there!' said Giles, mighty relieved. 'They're queer folk in those parts, I've heard tell, and aught might happen in their land. Let them get on with it! Don't come worriting me with such tales. Get out!'

Garm got out, and spread the news all over the

village. He did not forget to mention that his master was not scared in the least. 'Quite cool he was, and went on with his breakfast.'

People chatted about it pleasantly at their doors. 'How like old times!' they said. 'Just as Christmas is coming, too. So seasonable. How pleased the King will be! He will be able to have Real Tail this Christmas.'

But more news came in next day. The dragon, it appeared, was exceptionally large and ferocious. He was doing terrible damage.

'What about the King's knights?' people began to say.

Others had already asked the same question. Indeed, messengers were now reaching the King from the villages most afflicted by Chrysophylax, and they said to him as loudly and as often as they dared: 'Lord, what of your knights?'

But the knights did nothing; their knowledge of the dragon was still quite unofficial. So the King brought the matter to their notice, fully and formally, asking for necessary action at their early convenience. He was greatly displeased when he found that their convenience would not be early at all, and was indeed daily postponed.

Yet the excuse of the knights were undoubtedly sound. First of all, the Royal Cook had already made the Dragon's Tail for that Christmas, being a man who believed in getting things done in good time. It would not do at all to offend him by

23

bringing in a real tail at the last minute. He was a very valuable servant.

'Never mind the Tail! Cut his head off and put an end to him!' cried the messengers from the villages most nearly affected.

But Christmas had arrived, and most unfortunately a grand tournament had been arranged for St John's Day: knights of many realms had been invited and were coming to compete for a valuable prize. It was obviously unreasonable to spoil the chances of the Midland Knights by sending their best men off on a dragon-hunt before the tournament was over.

After that came the New Year Holiday.

But each night the dragon had moved; and each move had brought him nearer to Ham. On the night of New Year's Day people could see a blaze in the distance. The dragon had settled in a wood about ten miles away, and it was burning merrily. He was a hot dragon when he felt in the mood.

After that people began to look at Farmer Giles and whisper behind his back. It made him very uncomfortable; but he pretended not to notice it. The next day the dragon came several miles nearer. Then Farmer Giles himself began to talk loudly of the scandal of the King's knights.

'I should like to know what they do to earn their keep,' said he.

'So should we!' said everyone in Ham.

But the miller added: 'Some men still get knighthood by sheer merit, I am told. After all, our good Ægidius here is already a knight in a manner of speaking. Did not the King send him a red letter and a sword?'

'There's more to knighthood than a sword,' said Giles. 'There's dubbing and all that, or so I understand. Anyway I've my own business to attend to.'

'Oh! but the King would do the dubbing, I don't doubt, if he were asked,' said the miller. 'Let us ask him, before it is too late!'

'Nay!' said Giles. 'Dubbing is not for my sort. I am a farmer and proud of it: a plain honest man and honest men fare ill at court, they say. It is more in your line, Master Miller.'

The parson smiled: not at the farmer's retort, for Giles and the miller were always giving one another as good as they got, being bosom enemies, as the saying was in Ham. The parson had suddenly been struck with a notion that pleased him, but he said no more at that time. The miller was not so pleased, and he scowled.

'Plain certainly, and honest perhaps,' said he. 'But do you have to go to court and be a knight before you kill a dragon? Courage is all that is needed, as only yesterday I heard Master Ægidius declare. Surely he has as much courage as any knight?'

All the folk standing by shouted: 'Of course not!' and 'Yes indeed! Three cheers for the Hero of Ham!'

Then Farmer Giles went home feeling very uncomfortable. He was finding that a local reputation may require keeping up, and that may prove awkward. He kicked the dog, and hid the sword in a cupboard in the kitchen. Up till then it had hung over the fireplace.

The next day the dragon moved to the neighbouring village of Quercetum (Oakley in the vulgar tongue). He ate not only sheep and cows and one or two persons of tender age, but he ate the parson too. Rather rashly the parson had sought to dissuade him from his evil ways. Then there was a terrible commotion. All the people of Ham came up the hill headed by their own parson; and they waited on Farmer Giles.

'We look to you!' they said; and they remained standing round and looking, until the farmer's face was redder than his beard.

'When are you going to start?' they asked.

26

'Well, I can't start today, and that's a fact,' said he. 'I've a lot on hand with my cowman sick and all. I'll see about it.'

They went away; but in the evening it was rumoured that the dragon had moved even nearer, so they all came back.

'We look to you, Master Ægidius,' they said.

'Well,' said he, 'it's very awkward for me just now. My mare has gone lame, and the lambing has started. I'll see about it as soon as may be.'

So they went away once more, not without some grumbling and whispering. The miller was sniggering. The parson stayed behind, and could not be got rid of. He invited himself to supper, and made some pointed remarks. He even asked what had become of the sword and insisted on seeing it.

It was lying in a cupboard on a shelf hardly long enough for it, and as soon as Farmer Giles brought it out in a flash it leaped from the sheath, which the farmer dropped as if it had been hot. The parson sprang to his feet, upsetting his beer. He picked the sword up carefully and tried to put it back in the sheath; but it would not go so much as a foot in, and it jumped clean out again, as soon as he took his hand off the hilt.

'Dear me! This is very peculiar!' said the parson, and he took a good look at both scabbard and blade. He was a lettered man, but the farmer could only spell out large uncials with difficulty, and was none too sure of the reading even of his own name. That is why he had never given any

27

heed to the strange letters that could dimly be seen on sheath and sword. As for the King's armourer, he was so accustomed to runes, names, and other signs of power and significance upon swords and scabbards that he had not bothered his head about them; he thought them out of date, anyway.

But the parson looked long, and he frowned. He had expected to find some lettering on the sword or on the scabbard, and that was indeed the idea that had come to him the day before; but now he was surprised at what he saw, for letters and signs there were, to be sure, but he could not make head or tail of them.

'There is an inscription on this sheath, and some, ah, epigraphical signs are visible also upon the sword,' he said.

'Indeed?' said Giles. 'And what may that amount to?'

'The characters are archaic and the language barbaric,' said the parson, to gain time. 'A little closer inspection will be required.' He begged the loan of the sword for the night, and the farmer let him have it with pleasure.

When the parson got home he took down many learned books from his shelves, and he sat up far into the night. Next morning it was discovered that the dragon had moved nearer still. All the people of Ham barred their doors and shuttered their windows; and those that had cellars went down into them and sat shivering in the candle-light.

But the parson stole out and went from door to door; and he told, to all who would listen through a crack or a keyhole, what he had discovered in his study.

'Our good Ægidius,' he said, 'by the King's grace is now the owner of Caudimordax, the famous sword that in popular romances is more vulgarly called Tailbiter.'

Those that heard this name usually opened the door. They all knew the renown of Tailbiter, for that sword had belonged to Bellomarius, the greatest of all the dragon-slayers of the realm. Some accounts made him the maternal great-great-grandfather of the King. The songs and tales of his deeds were many, and if forgotten at court, were still remembered in the villages.

'This sword,' said the parson, 'will not stay sheathed, if a dragon is within five miles; and without doubt in a brave man's hands no dragon can resist it.'

Then people began to take heart again; and some unshuttered the windows and put their heads out. In the end the parson persuaded a few to come and join him; but only the miller was really willing. To see Giles in a real fix seemed to him worth the risk.

They went up the hill, not without anxious looks north across the river. There was no sign of the dragon. Probably he was asleep; he had been feeding very well all the Christmas-time.

The parson (and the miller) hammered on the farmer's door. There was no answer, so they hammered louder. At last Giles came out. His face was very red. He also had sat up far into the night, drinking a good deal of ale; and he had begun again as soon as he got up.

They all crowded round him, calling him Good Ægidius, Bold Ahenobarbus, Great Julius, Staunch Agricola, Pride of Ham, Hero of the Countryside. And they spoke of Caudimordax, Tailbiter, The Sword that would not be Sheathed, Death or Victory, The Glory of the Yeomanry, Backbone of the Country, and the Good of one's Fellow Men, until the farmer's head was hopelessly confused.

'Now then! One at a time!' he said, when he got a chance. 'What's all this, what's all this? It's my busy morning, you know.'

So they let the parson explain the situation. Then the miller had the pleasure of seeing the farmer in as tight a fix as he could wish. But things did not turn out quite as the miller expected. For one thing Giles had drunk a deal of strong ale. For another he had a queer feeling of pride and encouragement when he learned that his sword was actually Tailbiter. He had been very fond of tales about Bellomarius when he was a boy, and before he had learned sense he had sometimes wished that he could have a marvellous and heroic sword of his own. So it came over him all of a sudden that he would take Tailbiter and go dragon-hunting. But he had been used to bargaining all his life, and he made one more effort to postpone the event.

'What!' said he. 'Me go dragon-hunting? In my old leggings and waistcoat? Dragon-fights need some kind of armour, from all I've heard tell. There isn't any armour in this house, and that's a fact,' said he.

That was a bit awkward, they all allowed; but they sent for the blacksmith. The blacksmith shook his head. He was a slow, gloomy man, vulgarly known as Sunny Sam, though his proper name was Fabricus Cunctator. He never whistled at his work, unless some disaster (such as frost in May) had duly occurred after he had foretold it. Since he was daily foretelling disasters of every kind, few happened that he had not foretold, and he was able to take the credit of them. It was his chief pleasure; so naturally he was reluctant to do anything to avert them. He shook his head again.

'I can't make armour out of naught,' he said. 'And it's not in my line. You'd best get the carpenter to make you a wooden shield. Not that it will help you much. He's a hot dragon.'

Their faces fell; but the miller was not so easily to be turned from his plan of sending Giles to the dragon, if he would go; or of blowing the bubble of his local reputation, if he refused in the end. 'What about ring-mail?' he said. 'That would be a help; and it need not be very fine. It would be for business and not for showing off at court. What about your old leather jerkin, friend Ægidius? And there is a great pile of links and rings in the smithy. I don't suppose Master Fabricius himself knows what may be lying there.'

'You don't know what you are talking about,' said the smith, growing cheerful. 'If it's real ring-mail you mean, then you can't have it. It needs the skill of the dwarfs, with every little ring fitting into four others and all. Even if I had the craft, I should be working for weeks. And we shall all be in our graves before then,' said he, 'or leastways in the dragon.'

They all wrung their hands in dismay, and the blacksmith began to smile. But they were now so alarmed that they were unwilling to give up the miller's plan and they turned to him for counsel.

'Well,' said he, 'I've heard tell that in the old days those that could not buy bright hauberks out of the Southlands would stitch steel rings on a leather shirt and be content with that. Let's see what can be done in that line!'

So Giles had to bring out his old jerkin, and the smith was hurried back to his smithy. There they rummaged in every corner and turned over the pile of old metal, as had not been done for many a year. At the bottom they found, all dull with rust, a whole heap of small rings, fallen from some

forgotten coat, such as the miller had spoken of.
Sam, more unwilling and gloomy as the task
seemed more hopeful, was set to work on the
spot, gathering and sorting and cleaning the rings;
and when (as he was pleased to point out) these
were clearly insufficient for one so broad of back
and breast as Master Ægidius, they made him

split up old chains and hammer the links into
rings as fine as his skill could contrive.

They took the smaller rings of steel and stitched
them on to the breast of the jerkin, and the larger
and clumsier rings they stitched on the back; and
then, when still more rings were forthcoming, so
hard was poor Sam driven, they took a pair of the
farmer's breeches and stitched rings on to them.
And up on a shelf in a dark nook of the smithy the
miller found the old iron frame of a helmet, and
he set the cobbler to work, covering it with
leather as well as he could.

The work took them all the rest of that day, and
all the next day – which was Twelfthnight and the
eve of the Epiphany, but festivities were neg-
lected. Farmer Giles celebrated the occasion with
more ale than usual; but the dragon mercifully
slept. For the moment he had forgotten all about
hunger or swords.

Early on the Epiphany they went up the hill,
carrying the strange result of their handiwork.
Giles was expecting them. He had now no excuses left to offer; so he put on the mail jerkin and
the breeches. The miller sniggered. Then Giles
put on his topboots and an old pair of spurs; and
also the leather-covered helmet. But at the last
moment he clapped an old felt hat over the
helmet, and over the mail coat he threw his big
grey cloak.

'What is the purpose of that, Master?' they
asked.

'Well', said Giles, 'if it is your notion to go

34

dragon-hunting jingling and dingling like Canter-
bury Bells, it ain't mine. It don't seem sense to me
to let a dragon know that you are coming along
the road sooner than need be. And a helmet's a
helmet, and a challenge to battle. Let the worm
see only my old hat over the hedge, and maybe I'll
get nearer before the trouble begins.'

They had stitched on the rings so that they
overlapped, each hanging loose over the one
below, and jingle they certainly did. The cloak
did something to stop the noise of them, but Giles
cut a queer figure in his gear. They did not tell
him so. They girded the belt round his waist with
difficulty, and they hung the scabbard upon it; but
he had to carry the sword, for it would no longer
stay sheathed, unless held with main strength.

The farmer called for Garm. He was a just man
according to his lights. 'Dog,' he said, 'you are
coming with me.'

The dog howled. 'Help! help!' he cried.

'Now stop it!' said Giles. 'Or I'll give you
worse than any dragon could. You know the
smell of this worm, and maybe you'll prove
useful for once.'

Then Farmer Giles called for his grey mare. She
gave him a queer look and sniffed at the spurs.
But she let him get up; and then off they went,
and none of them felt happy. They trotted through
the village, and all the folk clapped and cheered,
mostly from their windows. The farmer and his
mare put as good a face on it as they could; but

Garm had no sense of shame and slunk along with his tail down.

They crossed the bridge over the river at the end of the village. When at last they were well out of sight, they slowed to a walk. Yet all too soon they passed out of the lands belonging to Farmer Giles and to other folk of Ham and came to parts that the dragon had visited. There were broken trees, burned hedges and blackened grass, and a nasty uncanny silence.

The sun was shining bright, and Farmer Giles began to wish that he dared shed a garment or two; and he wondered if he had not taken a pint too many. 'A nice end to Christmas and all,' he thought. 'And I'll be lucky if it don't prove the end of me too.' He mopped his face with a large handkerchief – green, not red; for red rags infuriate dragons, or so he had heard tell.

But he did not find the dragon. He rode down many lanes, wide and narrow, and over other farmers' deserted fields, and still he did not find the dragon. Garm was, of course, of no use at all. He kept just behind the mare and refused to use his nose.

They came at last to a winding road that had suffered little damage and seemed quiet and peaceful. After following it for half a mile Giles began to wonder whether he had not done his duty and all that his reputation required. He had made up his mind that he had looked long and far enough, and he was just thinking of turning back, and of his dinner, and of telling his friends that the

dragon had seen him coming and simply flown away, when he turned a sharp corner.

There was the dragon, lying half across a broken hedge with his horrible head in the middle of the road. 'Help!' said Garm and bolted. The grey mare sat down plump, and Farmer Giles went off backwards into a ditch. When he put his head out, there was the dragon wide awake looking at him.

'Good morning!' said the dragon. 'You seem surprised.'

'Good morning!' said Giles. 'I am that.'

'Excuse me,' said the dragon. He had cocked a very suspicious ear when he caught the sound of rings jingling, as the farmer fell. 'Excuse my asking, but were you looking for me, by any chance?'

'No, indeed!' said the farmer. 'Who'd a' thought of seeing you here? I was just going for a ride.'

He scrambled out of the ditch in a hurry and backed away towards the grey mare. She was now on her feet again and was nibbling some grass at the wayside, seeming quite unconcerned.

'Then we meet by good luck,' said the dragon. 'The pleasure is mine. Those are your holiday clothes, I suppose. A new fashion, perhaps?' Farmer Giles's felt hat had fallen off and his grey cloak had slipped open; but he brazened it out.

'Aye,' said he, 'brand-new. But I must be after that dog of mine. He's gone after rabbits, I fancy.'

'I fancy not,' said Chrysophylax, licking his lips

(a sign of amusement). 'He will get home a long time before you do, I expect. But pray proceed on your way, Master – let me see, I don't think I know your name?'

'Nor I yours,' said Giles; 'and we'll leave it at that.'

'As you like,' said Chrysophylax, licking his lips again, but pretending to close his eyes. He had a wicked heart (as dragons all have), but not a very bold one (as is not unusual). He preferred a meal that he did not have to fight for; but appetite had returned after a good long sleep. The parson of Oakley had been stringy, and it was years since he had tasted a large fat man. He had now made up his mind to try this easy meat, and he was only waiting until the old fool was off his guard.

But the old fool was not as foolish as he looked, and he kept his eye on the dragon, even while he was trying to mount. The mare, however, had other ideas, and she kicked and shied when Giles tried to get up. The dragon became impatient and made ready to spring.

'Excuse me!' said he. 'Haven't you dropped something?'

An ancient trick, but it succeeded; for Giles had indeed dropped something. When he fell he had dropped Caudimordax (or vulgar Tailbiter), and there it lay by the wayside. He stooped to pick it up; and the dragon sprang. But not as quick as Tailbiter. As soon as it was in the farmer's hand, it leaped forward with a flash, straight at the dragon's eyes.

'Hey!' said the dragon, and stopped very short. 'What have you got there?'

'Only Tailbiter, that was given to me by the King,' said Giles.

'My mistake!' said the dragon. 'I beg your pardon.' He lay and grovelled, and Farmer Giles began to feel more comfortable. 'I don't think you have treated me fair.'

'How not?' said Giles. 'And anyway why should I?'

'You have concealed your honourable name and pretended that our meeting was by chance; yet you are plainly a knight of high lineage. It used, sir, to be the custom of knights to issue a challenge in such cases, after a proper exchange of titles and credentials.'

'Maybe it used, and maybe it still is,' said Giles, beginning to feel pleased with himself. A man who has a large and imperial dragon grovelling before him may be excused if he feels somewhat uplifted. 'But you are making more mistakes than one, old worm. I am no knight. I am Farmer Ægidius of Ham, I am; and I can't abide trespassers. I've shot giants with my blunderbuss before now, for doing less damage than you have. And I issued no challenge neither.'

The dragon was disturbed. 'Curse that giant for a liar!' he thought. 'I have been sadly misled. And now what on earth does one do with a bold farmer and a sword so bright and aggressive?' He could recall no precedent for such a situation. 'Chrysophylax is my name,' said he, 'Chrysophylax the Rich. What can I do for your honour?' he added ingratiatingly, with one eye on the sword, and hoping to escape battle.

'You can take yourself off, you horny old varmint,' said Giles, also hoping to escape battle. 'I only want to be shut of you. Go right away from here, and get back to your own dirty den!' He stepped towards Chrysophylax, waving his arms as if he was scaring crows.

That was quite enough for Tailbiter. It circled flashing in the air; then down it came, smiting the dragon on the joint of the right wing, a ringing blow that shocked him exceedingly. Of course Giles knew very little about the right methods of killing a dragon, or the sword might have landed in a tenderer spot; but Tailbiter did the best it could in inexperienced hands. It was quite enough for Chrysophylax – he could not use the wing for days. Up he got and turned to fly, and found that he could not. The farmer sprang on the mare's back. The dragon began to run. So did the mare. The dragon galloped over a field puffing and blowing. So did the mare. The farmer bawled and shouted, as if he was watching a horse race; and all the while he waved Tailbiter. The faster the dragon ran the more bewildered he became; and all the while the grey mare put her best leg foremost and kept close behind him.

On they pounded down the lanes, and through the gaps in the fences, over many fields and across many brooks. The dragon was smoking and bellowing and losing all sense of direction. At last

41

they came suddenly to the bridge of Ham, thundered over it, and came roaring down the village street. There Garm had the impudence to sneak out of an alley and join in the chase.

All the people were at their windows or on the roofs. Some laughed and some cheered; and some beat tins and pans and kettles; and others blew horns and pipes and whistles; and the parson had the church bells rung. Such a to-do and an ongoing had not been heard in Ham for a hundred years.

Just outside the church the dragon gave up. He lay down in the middle of the road and gasped. Garm came and sniffed at his tail, but Chrysophylax was past all shame.

'Good people, and gallant warrior,' he panted, as Farmer Giles rode up, while the villagers gathered round (at a reasonable distance) with hayforks, poles, and pokers in their hands. 'Good people, don't kill me! I am very rich. I will pay for all the damage I have done. I will pay for the funerals of all the people I have killed, especially the parson of Oakley; he shall have a noble cenotaph – though he was rather lean. I will give you each a really good present, if you will only let me go home and fetch it.'

'How much?' said the farmer.

'Well,' said the dragon, calculating quickly. He noticed that the crowd was rather large. 'Thirteen and eightpence each?'

'Nonesense!' said Giles. 'Rubbish!' said the people. 'Rot!' said the dog.

'Two golden guineas each, and children half price?' said the dragon.

'What about dogs?' said Garm. 'Go on!' said the farmer. 'We're listening.'

'Ten pounds and a purse of silver for every soul, and gold collars for the dogs?' said Chrysophylax anxiously.

'Kill him!' shouted the people, getting impatient.

'A bag of gold for everybody, and diamonds for the ladies?' said Chrysophylax hurriedly.

'Now you're talking, but not good enough,' said Farmer Giles. 'You've left dogs out again,' said Garm. 'What size of bags?' said the men. 'How many diamonds?' said their wives.

'Dear me! dear me!' said the dragon. 'I shall be ruined.'

'You deserve it,' said Giles. 'You can choose between being ruined and being killed where you lie.' He brandished Tailbiter, and the dragon cowered. 'Make up your mind!' the people cried, getting bolder and drawing nearer.

Chrysophylax blinked; but deep down inside him he laughed: a silent quiver which they did not observe. Their bargaining had begun to amuse him. Evidently they expected to get something out of it. They knew very little of the ways of the wide and wicked world – indeed, there was no one now living in all the realm who had had any actual experience in dealing with dragons and their tricks. Chrysophylax was getting his breath back, and his wits as well. He licked his lips.

'Name your own price!' he said.

Then they all began to talk at once. Chrysophy-lax listened with interest. Only one voice disturbed him: that of the blacksmith.

'No good'll come of it, mark my words,' said he. 'A worm won't return, say what you like. But no good will come of it, either way.'

'You can stand out of the bargain, if that's your mind,' they said to him, and went on haggling, taking little further notice of the dragon.

Chrysophylax raised his head; but if he thought of springing on them, or of slipping off during the argument he was disappointed. Farmer Giles was standing by, chewing a straw and considering; but Tailbiter was in his hand, and his eye was on the dragon.

'You lie where you be!' said he, 'or you'll get what you deserve, gold or no gold.'

The dragon lay flat. At last the parson was made spokesman and he stepped up beside Giles. 'Vile Worm!' he said. 'You must bring back to this spot all your ill-gotten wealth; and after recompensing those whom you have injured we will share it fairly among ourselves. Then, if you make a solemn vow never to disturb our land again, nor to stir up any other monster to trouble us, we will let you depart with both your head and your tail to your own home. And now you shall take such strong oaths to return (with your ransoms) as even the conscience of a worm must hold binding.'

Chrysophylax accepted, after a plausible show

of hesitation. He even shed hot tears, lamenting his ruin, till there were steaming puddles in the road; but no one was moved by them. He swore many oaths, solemn and astonishing, that he would return with all his wealth on the feast of St Hilarius and St Felix. That gave him eight days, and far too short a time for the journey, as even those ignorant of geography might well have reflected. Nonetheless they let him go, and escorted him as far as the bridge.

'To our next meeting!' he said, as he passed over the river. 'I am sure we shall all look forward to it.'

'We shall indeed,' they said. They were, of course, very foolish. For though the oaths he had taken should have burdened his conscience with sorrow and a great fear of disaster, he had, alas! no conscience at all. And if this regrettable lack in

one of imperial lineage was beyond the comprehension of the simple, at the least the parson with his booklearning might have guessed it. Maybe he did. He was a grammarian, and could doubtless see further into the future than others.

The blacksmith shook his head as he went back to his smithy. 'Ominous names,' he said. 'Hilarius and Felix! I don't like the sound of them.'

The King, of course, quickly heard the news. It ran through the realm like fire and lost nothing in the telling. The King was deeply moved, for various reasons, not the least being financial; and he made up his mind to ride at once in person to Ham, where such strange things seemed to happen.

He arrived four days after the dragon's departure, coming over the bridge on his white horse, with many knights and trumpeters, and a large

47

baggage-train. All the people had put on their best clothes and lined the street to welcome him. The cavalcade came to a halt in the open space before the church gate. Farmer Giles knelt before the King, when he was presented; but the King told him to rise, and actually patted him on the back. The knights pretended not to observe this familiarity.

The King ordered the whole village to assemble in Farmer Giles's large pasture beside the river; and when they were all gathered together (including Garm, who felt that he was concerned), Augustus Bonifacius rex et basileus was graciously pleased to address them.

He explained carefully that the wealth of the miscreant Chrysophylax all belonged to himself as lord of the land. He passed rather lightly over his claim to be considered suzerain of the mountain-country (which was debatable); but 'we make no doubt in any case,' said he, 'that all the treasure of this worm was stolen from our ancestors. Yet we are, as all know, both just and generous, and our good liege Ægidius shall be suitably rewarded; nor shall any of our loyal subjects in this place go without some token of our esteem, from the parson to the youngest child. For we are well pleased with Ham. Here at least a sturdy and uncorrupted folk still retain the ancient courage of our race.' The knights were talking among themselves about the new fashion in hats.

The people bowed and curtsied, and thanked

him humbly. But they wished now that they had closed with the dragon's offer of ten pounds all round, and kept the matter private. They knew enough, at any rate, to feel sure that the King's esteem would not rise to that. Garm noticed that there was no mention of dogs. Farmer Giles was the only one of them who was really content. He felt sure of some reward, and was mighty glad anyway to have come safely out of a nasty business with his local reputation higher than ever.

The King did not go away. He pitched his pavilions in Farmer Giles's field, and waited for January the fourteenth, making as merry as he could in a miserable village far from the capital. The royal retinue ate up nearly all the bread, butter, eggs, chickens, bacon and mutton, and drank up every drop of old ale there was in the place in the next three days. Then they began to grumble at short commons. But the King paid handsomely for everything (in tallies to be honoured later by the Exchequer, which he hoped would shortly be richly replenished); so the folk of Ham were well satisfied, not knowing the actual state of the Exchequer.

January the fourteenth came, the feast of Hilarius and of Felix, and everybody was up and about early. The knights put on their armour. The farmer put on his coat of home-made mail, and they smiled openly, until they caught the King's frown. The farmer also put on Tailbiter, and it

went into its sheath as easy as butter, and stayed there. The parson looked hard at the sword, and nodded to himself. The blacksmith laughed.

Midday came. People were too anxious to eat much. The afternoon passed slowly. Still Tailbiter showed no sign of leaping from the scabbard. None of the watchers on the hill, nor any of the small boys who had climbed to the tops of tall trees, could see anything by air or by land that might herald the return of the dragon.

The blacksmith walked about whistling; but it was not until evening fell and the stars came out that the other folk of the village began to suspect that the dragon did not mean to come back at all. Still they recalled his many solemn and astonishing oaths and kept on hoping. When, however, midnight struck and the appointed day was over, their disappointment was deep. The blacksmith was delighted.

'I told you so,' he said. But they were still not convinced.

'After all he was badly hurt,' said some.

'We did not give him enough time,' said others. 'It is a powerful long way to the mountains, and he would have a lot to carry. Maybe he has had to get help.'

But the next day passed and the next. Then they all gave up hope. The King was in a red rage. The victuals and drink had run out, and the knights were grumbling loudly. They wished to go back to the merriments of court. But the King wanted money.

51

He took leave of his loyal subjects, but he was short and sharp about it; and he cancelled half the tallies on the Exchequer. He was quite cold to Farmer Giles and dismissed him with a nod.

'You will hear from us later,' he said, and rode off with his knights and his trumpeters.

The more hopeful and simple-minded thought that a message would soon come from the court to summon Master Ægidius to the King, to be knighted at the least. In a week the message came, but it was of different sort. It was written and signed in triplicate: one copy for Giles; one for the parson; and one to be nailed on the church door. Only the copy addressed to the parson was of any use, for the court-hand was peculiar and as dark to the folk of Ham as the Book-latin. But the parson rendered it into the vulgar tongue and read it from the pulpit. It was short and to the point (for a royal letter); the King was in a hurry.

'We Augustus B. A. A. P and M. rex et cetera make known that we have determined, for the safety of our realm and for the keeping of our honour, that the worm or dragon styling himself Chrysophylax the Rich shall be sought out and condignly punished for his misdemeanours, torts, felonies, and foul perjury. All the knights of our Royal Household are hereby commanded to arm and make ready to ride upon this quest, so soon as Master Aegidius A. J. Agricola shall arrive at this our court. Inasmuch as the said Aegidius has proved himself a trusty man and well able to deal with giants, dragons, and other enemies of the

52

𝕶ing's peace, now therefore we command him to ride forth
at once, and to join the company of our knights with all
speed.'

People said this was a high honour and next
door to being dubbed. The miller was envious.
'Friend Ægidius is rising in the world,' said he. 'I
hope he will know us when he gets back.'

'Maybe he never will,' said the blacksmith.

'That's enough from you, old horse-face!' said
the farmer, mighty put out. 'Honour be blowed!
If I get back even the miller's company will be
welcome. Still, it is some comfort to think that I
shall be missing you both for a bit.' And with that
he left them.

You cannot offer excuses to the King as you can
to your neighbours; so lambs or no lambs,
ploughing or none, milk or water, he had to get
up on his grey mare and go. The parson saw him
off.

'I hope you are taking some stout rope with
you?' he said.

'What for?' said Giles. 'To hang myself?'

'Nay! Take heart, Master Ægidius!' said the
parson. 'It seems to me that you have a luck that
you can trust. But take also a long rope, for you
may need it, unless my foresight deceives me.
And now farewell, and return safely!'

'Aye! And come back and find all my house and
land in a pickle. Blast dragons!' said Giles. Then,
stuffing a great coil of rope in a bag by his saddle,
he climbed up and rode off.

He did not take the dog, who had kept well out of sight all the morning. But when he was gone, Garm slunk home and stayed there, and howled all the night, and was beaten for it, and went on howling.

'Help, ow help!' he cried. 'I'll never see dear master again, and he was so terrible and splendid. I wish I had gone with him, I do.'

'Shut up!' said the farmer's wife, 'or you'll never live to see if he comes back or he don't.'

The blacksmith heard the howls. 'A bad omen,' he said cheerfully.

Many days passed and no news came. 'No news is bad news,' he said, and burst into song.

When Farmer Giles got to court he was tired and dusty. But the knights, in polished mail and with shining helmets on their heads, were all standing by their horses. The King's summons and the inclusion of the farmer had annoyed them, and so they insisted on obeying orders literally, setting off the moment that Giles arrived. The poor farmer had barely time to swallow a sop in a draught of wine before he was off on the road again. The mare was offended. What she thought of the King was luckily unexpressed, as it was highly disloyal.

It was already late in the day. 'Too late in the day to start a dragon-hunt,' thought Giles. But they did not go far. The knights were in no hurry, once they had started. They rode along at their leisure, in a straggling line, knights, esquires, servants, and ponies trussed with baggage; and Farmer Giles jogging behind on his tired mare.

When evening came, they halted and pitched their tents. No provision had been made for Farmer Giles and he had to borrow what he could. The mare was indignant, and she forswore her allegiance to the house of Augustus Bonifacius.

The next day they rode on, and all the day after. On the third day they descried in the distance the dim and inhospitable mountains. Before long they were in regions where the lordship of Augustus Bonifacius was not universally acknowledged. They rode then with more care and kept closer together.

On the fourth day they reached the Wild Hills and the borders of the dubious lands where legendary creatures were reputed to dwell. Suddenly one of those riding ahead came upon ominous footprints in the sand by a stream. They called for the farmer.

'What are these, Master Ægidius?' they said.

'Dragon-marks,' said he.

'Lead on!' said they.

So now they rode west with Farmer Giles at their head, and all the rings were jingling on his leather coat. That mattered little; for all the knights were laughing and talking, and a minstrel rode with them singing a lay. Every now and again they took up the refrain of the song and sang it all together, very loud and strong. It was encouraging, for the song was good – it had been made long before in days when battles were more common than tournaments; but it was unwise. Their coming was now known to all the creatures of that land, and the dragons were cocking their ears in all the caves of the West. There was no longer any chance of their catching old Chrysophylax napping.

As luck (or the grey mare herself) would have it, when at last they drew under the very shadow of the dark mountains, Farmer Giles's mare went lame. They had now begun to ride along steep and stony paths, climbing upwards with toil and ever-growing disquiet. Bit by bit she dropped back in the line, stumbling and limping and looking so patient and sad that at last Farmer Giles was obliged to get off and walk. Soon they found themselves right at the back among the pack-ponies; but no one took any notice of them. The knights were discussing points of precedence and etiquette, and their attention was distracted. Otherwise they would have observed that dragon-marks were now obvious and numerous.

They had come, indeed, to the places where Chrysophylax often roamed, or alighted after taking his daily exercise in the air. The lower hills, and the slopes on either side of the path, had a scorched and trampled look. There was little grass, and the twisted stumps of heather and gorse stood up black amid wide patches of ash and burned earth. The region had been a dragons' playground for many a year. A dark mountain-wall loomed up before them.

Farmer Giles was concerned about his mare; but he was glad of the excuse for no longer being so conspicuous. It had not pleased him to be riding at the head of such a cavalcade in these dreary and dubious places. A little later he was gladder still, and had reason to thank his fortune (and his mare). For just about midday – it being then the Feast of Candlemas, and the seventh day of their riding – Tailbiter leaped out of its sheath, and the dragon out of his cave.

Without warning or formality he swooped out to give battle. Down he came upon them with a rush and a roar. Far from his home he had not shown himself over bold, in spite of his ancient and imperial lineage. But now he was filled with a great wrath; for he was fighting at his own gate, as it were, and with all his treasure to defend. He came round a shoulder of the mountain like a ton of thunderbolts, with a noise like a gale and a gust of red lightning.

The argument concerning precedence stopped short. All the horses shied to one side or the other,

57

and some of the knights fell off. The ponies and the baggage and the servants turned and ran at once. They had no doubt as to the order of precedence.

Suddenly there came a rush of smoke that smothered them all, and right in the midst of it the dragon crashed into the head of the line. Several of the knights were killed before they could even issue their formal challenge to battle, and several others were bowled over, horses and all. As for the remainder, their steeds took charge of them, and turned round and fled, carrying their masters off, whether they wished it or no. Most of them wished it indeed.

But the old grey mare did not budge. Maybe she was afraid of breaking her legs on the steep stony path. Maybe she felt too tired to run away. She knew in her bones that dragons on the wing are worse behind you than before you, and you need more speed than a race-horse for flight to be useful. Besides, she had seen this Chrysophylax before, and remembered chasing him over field and brook in her own country, till he lay down tame in the village high-street. Anyway she stuck her legs out wide, and she snorted. Farmer Giles went as pale as his face could manage, but he stayed by her side; for there seemed nothing else to do.

And so it was that the dragon, charging down the line, suddenly saw straight in front of him his old enemy with Tailbiter in his hand. It was the last thing he expected. He swerved aside like a great bat and collapsed on the hillside close to the road. Up came the grey mare, quite forgetting to walk lame. Farmer Giles, much encouraged, had scrambled hastily on her back.

'Excuse me,' said he, 'but were you looking for me, by any chance?'

'No, indeed!' said Chrysophylax. 'Who would have thought of seeing you here? I was just flying about.'

'Then we meet by good luck,' said Giles, 'and the pleasure is mine; for I was looking for *you*. What's more, I have a bone to pick with you, several bones in a manner of speaking.'

The dragon snorted. Farmer Giles put up his arm to ward off the hot gust, and with a flash Tailbiter swept forward, dangerously near the dragon's nose.

'Hey!' said he, and stopped snorting. He began to tremble and backed away, and all the fire in him was chilled. 'You have not, I hope, come to kill me, good master?' he whined.

'Nay! nay!' said the farmer. 'I said naught about killing.' The grey mare sniffed.

'Then what, may I ask, are you doing with all these knights?' said Chrysophylax. 'Knights always kill dragons, if we don't kill them first.'

'I'm doing nothing with them at all. They're naught to me,' said Giles. 'And anyway, they are all dead now or gone. What about what you said last Epiphany?'

'What about it?' said the dragon anxiously.

'You're nigh on a month late,' said Giles, 'and payment is overdue. I've come to collect it. You should beg my pardon for all the bother I have been put to.'

'I do indeed!' said he. 'I wish you had not troubled to come.'

'It'll be every bit of your treasure this time, and no market-tricks,' said Giles, 'or dead you'll be, and I shall hang your skin from our church steeple as a warning.'

'It's cruel hard!' said the dragon.

'A bargain's a bargain,' said Giles.

'Can't I keep just a ring or two, and a mite of gold, in consideration of cash payment?' said he.

'Not a brass button!' said Giles. And so they kept on for a while, chaffering and arguing like folk at a fair. Yet the end of it was as you might expect; for whatever else might be said, few had ever outlasted Farmer Giles at a bargaining.

The dragon had to walk all the way back to his cave, for Giles stuck to his side with Tailbiter held mighty close. There was a narrow path that wound up and round the mountain, and there was barely room for the two of them. The mare came just behind and she looked rather thoughtful.

It was five miles, if it was a step, and stiff going: and Giles trudged along, puffing and blowing, but never taking his eye off the worm. At last on the west side of the mountain they came to the mouth of the cave. It was large and black and forbidding, and its brazen doors swung on great pillars of iron. Plainly it had been a place of strength and pride in days long forgotten; for dragons do not build such works nor delve such mines, but dwell rather, when they may, in the tombs and treasuries of mighty men and giants of old. The doors of this deep house were set wide, and in their shadow they halted. So far Chrysophylax had had no chance to escape, but coming now to his own gate he sprang forward and prepared to plunge in.

Farmer Giles hit him with the flat of the sword. 'Woa!' said he. 'Before you go in, I've something to say to you. If you ain't outside again in quick time with something worth bringing, I shall come in after you and cut off your tail to begin with.'

The mare sniffed. She could not imagine Farmer Giles going down alone into a dragon's den for any money on earth. But Chrysophylax was quite prepared to believe it, with Tailbiter looking so bright and sharp and all. And maybe he was right, and the mare, for all her wisdom, had not yet understood the change in her master. Farmer Giles was backing his luck, and after two encounters was beginning to fancy that no dragon could stand up to him.

Anyway, out came Chrysophylax again in mighty quick time, with twenty pounds (troy) of gold and silver, and a chest of rings and necklaces and other pretty stuff.

'There!' said he.

'Where?' said Giles. 'That's not half enough, if that's what you mean. Nor half what you've got, I'll be bound.'

'Of course not!' said the dragon, rather perturbed to find that the farmer's wits seemed to have become brighter since that day in the village. 'Of course not! But I can't bring it all out at once.'

'Nor at twice, I'll wager,' said Giles. 'In you go again and out again double quick, or I'll give you a taste of Tailbiter!'

'No!' said the dragon, and in he popped and out again double quick. 'There!' said he, putting down an enormous load of gold and two chests of diamonds.

'Now try again!' said the farmer, 'And try harder!'

'It's hard, cruel hard,' said the dragon, as he went back in again.

But by this time the grey mare was getting a bit anxious on her own account. 'Who's going to carry all this heavy stuff home, I wonder?' thought she; and she gave such a long sad look at all the bags and the boxes that the farmer guessed her mind.

'Never you worry, lass!' 'We'll make the old worm do the carting.'

'Mercy on us!' said the dragon, who overheard these words as he came out of the cave for the third time with the biggest load of all, and a mort of rich jewels like green and red fire. 'Mercy on us! If I carry all this, it will be near the death of me, and a bag more I never could manage, not if you killed me for it.'

'Then there is more still, is there?' said the farmer.

'Yes,' said the dragon, 'enough to keep me respectable.' He spoke near the truth for a rare wonder, and wisely as it turned out. 'If you will leave me what remains,' said he very wily, 'I'll be your friend for ever. And I will carry all this treasure back to your honour's own house and not to the King's. And I will help you to keep it, what is more,' said he.

Then the farmer took out a toothpick with his left hand, and he thought very hard for a minute. Then 'Done with you!' he said, showing a laudable discretion. A knight would have stood out for the whole hoard and got a curse laid upon it. And as likely as not, if Giles had driven the worm to despair, he would have turned and fought in the end, Tailbiter or no Tailbiter. In which case Giles, if not slain himself, would have been obliged to slaughter his transport and leave the best part of his gains in the mountains.

Well, that was the end of it. The farmer stuffed his pockets with jewels, just in case anything went wrong; and he gave the grey mare a small load to carry. All the rest he bound on the back of

Chrysophylax in boxes and bags, till he looked like a royal pantechnicon. There was no chance of his flying, for his load was too great, and Giles had tied down his wings.

'Mighty handy this rope has turned out in the end!' he thought, and he remembered the parson with gratitude.

So off now the dragon trotted, puffing and blowing, with the mare at his tail, and the farmer holding out Caudimordax very bright and threatening. He dared try no tricks.

In spite of their burdens the mare and the dragon made better speed going back than the cavalcade had made coming. For Farmer Giles was in a hurry – not the least reason being that he had little food in his bags. Also he had no trust in Chrysophylax after his breaking of oaths so solemn and binding, and he wondered much how to get through a night without death or great loss. But before that night fell he ran again into luck; for they overtook half a dozen of the servants and ponies that had departed in haste and were now wandering at a loss in the Wild Hills. They scattered in fear and amazement, but Giles shouted after them.

'Hey, lads!' said he. 'Come back! I have a job for you, and good wages while this packet lasts.'

So they entered his service, being glad of a guide, and thinking that their wages might indeed come more regular now than had been usual. Then they rode on, seven men, six ponies, one mare, and a dragon; and Giles began to feel like a lord and stuck out his chest. They halted as seldom as they could. At night Farmer Giles roped the dragon to four pickets, one to each leg, with three men to watch him in turn. But the grey mare kept half an eye open, in case the men should try any tricks on their own account.

After three days they were back over the borders of their own country; and their arrival caused such wonder and uproar as had seldom been seen between the two seas before. In the first village that they stopped at food and drink was showered on them free, and half the young lads wanted to join in the procession. Giles chose out a dozen likely young fellows. He promised them good wages, and bought them such mounts as he could get. He was beginning to have ideas.

After resting a day he rode on again, with his new escort at his heels. They sang songs in his honour: rough and ready, but they sounded good in his ears. Some folk cheered and others laughed. It was a sight both merry and wonderful.

Soon Farmer Giles took a bend southward, and steered towards his own home, and never went near the court of the King nor sent any message. But the news of the return of Master Ægidius spread like fire from the West; and there was great astonishment and confusion. For he came hard on the heels of a royal proclamation bidding all the towns and villages to go into mourning for the fall of the brave knights in the pass of the mountains.

Wherever Giles went the mourning was cast aside, and bells were set ringing, and people thronged by the wayside shouting and waving their caps and their scarves. But they booed the poor dragon, till he began bitterly to regret the bargain he had made. It was most humiliating for one of ancient and imperial lineage. When they got back to Ham all the dogs barked at him scornfully. All except Garm: he had eyes, ears, and nose only for his master. Indeed, he went quite off his head, and turned somersaults all along the street.

Ham, of course, gave the farmer a wonderful welcome; but probably nothing pleased him more than finding the miller at a loss for a sneer and the blacksmith quite out of countenance.

'This is not the end of the affair, mark my words!' said he; but he could not think of anything worse to say and hung his head gloomily. Farmer Giles, with his six men and his dozen likely lads and the dragon and all, went on up the hill, and there they stayed quiet for a while. Only the parson was invited to the house.

The news soon reached the capital, and forgetting the official mourning, and their business as well, people gathered in the streets. There was much shouting and noise.

The King was in his great house, biting his nails and tugging his beard. Between grief and rage (and financial anxiety) his mood was so grim that no one dared speak to him. But at last the noise of the town came to his ears; it did not sound like mourning or weeping.

'What is all the noise about?' he demanded. 'Tell the people to go indoors and mourn decently! It sounds more like a goose-fair.'

'The dragon has come back, lord,' they answered.

'What!' said the King. 'Summon our knights, or what is left of them!'

'There is no need, lord,' they answered. 'With Master Ægidius behind him the dragon is tame as tame. Or so we are informed. The news has not long come in, and reports are conflicting.'

'Bless our Soul!' said the King, looking greatly relieved. 'And to think that we ordered a Dirge to be sung for the fellow the day after tomorrow! Cancel it! Is there any sign of our treasure?'

'Reports say that there is veritable mountain of it, lord,' they answered.

'When will it arrive?' said the King eagerly. 'A good man this Ægidius – send him in to us as soon as he comes!'

There was some hesitation in replying to this. At last someone took courage and said: 'Your pardon, lord, but we hear that the farmer has turned aside towards his own home. But doubtless he will hasten here in suitable raiment at the earliest opportunity.'

'Doubtless,' said the King. 'But confound his raiment! He had no business to go home without reporting. We are much displeased.'

The earliest opportunity presented itself, and passed, and so did many later ones. In fact, Farmer Giles had been back for a good week or more, and still no word or news of him came to the court.

On the tenth day the King's rage exploded. 'Send for the fellow!' he said; and they sent. It was a day's hard riding to Ham, each way.

'He will not come, lord!' said a trembling messenger two days later.

'Lightning of Heaven!' said the King. 'Command him to come on Tuesday next, or he shall be cast into prison for life!'

'Your pardon, lord, but he still will not come,' said a truly miserable messenger returning alone on the Tuesday.

'Ten Thousand Thunders!' said the King. 'Take this fool to prison instead! Now send some men to fetch the churl in chains!' he bellowed to those that stood by.

'How many men?' they faltered. 'There's a dragon, and . . . and Tailbiter, and—'

'And broomstales and fiddlesticks!' said the King. Then he ordered his white horse, and summoned his knights (or what was left of them) and a company of men-at-arms, and he rode off in fiery anger. All the people ran out of their houses in surprise.

But Farmer Giles had now become more than the Hero of the Countryside: he was the Darling of the Land; and folk did not cheer the knights and men-at-arms as they went by, though they still took off their hats to the King. As he drew nearer to Ham the looks grew more sullen; in some villages the people shut their doors and not a face could be seen.

Then the King changed from hot wrath to cold anger. He had a grim look as he rode up at last to the river beyond which lay Ham and the house of the farmer. He had a mind to burn the place down. But there was Farmer Giles on the bridge, sitting on the grey mare with Tailbiter in his hand. No one else was to be seen, except Garm, who was lying in the road.

'Good morning, lord!' said Giles, as cheerful as day, not waiting to be spoken to.

The King eyed him coldly. 'Your manners are unfit for our presence,' said he; 'but that does not excuse you from coming when sent for.'

'I had not thought of it, lord, and that's a fact,' said Giles. 'I had matters of my own to mind, and had wasted time enough on your errands.'

'Ten Thousand Thunders!' cried the King in a hot rage again. 'To the devil with you and your insolence! No reward will you get after this; and you will be lucky if you escape hanging. And hanged you shall be, unless you beg

70

our pardon here and now, and give us back our sword.'

'Eh?' said Giles. 'I have got my reward, I reckon. Finding's keeping, and keeping's having, we say here. And I reckon Tailbiter is better with me than with your folk. But what are all these knights and men for, by any chance?' he asked. 'If you've come on a visit, you'd be welcome with fewer. If you want to take me away, you'll need a lot more.'

The King choked, and the knights went very red and looked down their noses. Some of the men-at-arms grinned, since the King's back was turned to them.

'Give me my sword!' shouted the King, finding his voice, but forgetting his plural.

'Give us your crown!' said Giles: a staggering remark, such as had never before been heard in all the days of the Middle Kingdom.

'Lightning of Heaven! Seize him and bind him!' cried the King, justly enraged beyond bearing. 'What do you hang back for? Seize him or slay him!'

The men-at-arms strode forward.

'Help! help! help! cried Garm.

Just at that moment the dragon got up from under the bridge. He had lain there concealed under the far bank, deep in the river. Now he let off a terrible steam, for he had drunk many gallons of water. At once there was a thick fog, and only the red eyes of the dragon to be seen in it.

71

'Go home, you fools!' he bellowed. 'Or I will tear you to pieces. There are knights lying cold in the mountain-pass, and soon there will be more in the river. All the King's horses and all the King's men!' he roared.

Then he sprang forward and struck a claw into the King's white horse; and it galloped away like the ten thousand thunders that the King mentioned so often. The other horses followed as swiftly: some had met this dragon before and did not like the memory. The men-at-arms legged it as best they could in every direction save that of Ham.

The white horse was only scratched, and he was not allowed to go far. After a while the King brought him back. He was master of his own horse at any rate; and no one could say that he was afraid of any man or dragon on the face of the earth. The fog was gone when he got back, but so were all his knights and his men. Now things looked very different with the King all alone to talk to a stout farmer with Tailbiter and a dragon as well.

But talk did no good. Farmer Giles was obstinate. He would not yield, and he would not fight, though the King challenged him to single combat there and then.

'Nay, lord!' said he, laughing. 'Go home and get cool! I don't want to hurt you; but you had best be off, or I won't be answerable for the worm. Good day!'

And that was the end of the Battle of the Bridge

of Ham. Never a penny of all the treasure did the King get, nor any word of apology from Farmer Giles, who was beginning to think mighty well of himself. What is more, from that day the power of the Middle Kingdom came to an end in that neighbourhood. For many a mile round about men took Giles for their lord. Never a man could the King with all his titles get to ride against the rebel Ægidius; for he had become the Darling of the Land, and the matter of song; and it was impossible to suppress all the lays that celebrated his deeds. The favourite one dealt with the meeting on the bridge in a hundred mock-heroic couplets.

Chrysophylax remained long in Ham, much to the profit of Giles; for the man who has a tame dragon is naturally respected. He was housed in the tithebarn, with the leave of the parson, and there he was guarded by the twelve likely lads. In this way arose the first of the titles of Giles: Dominus de Domito Serpente, which is in the vulgar Lord of the Tame Worm, or shortly of Tame. As such he was widely honoured; but he still paid a nominal tribute to the King: six oxtails and a pint of bitter, delivered on St Matthias' Day, that being the date of the meeting on the bridge. Before long, however, he advanced the Lord to Earl, and the belt of the Earl of Tame was indeed of great length.

After some years he became Prince Julius Ægidius and the tribute ceased. For Giles, being fabulously rich, had built himself a hall of great

74

magnificence, and gathered great strength of men-at-arms. Very bright and gay they were, for their gear was the best that money could buy. Each of the twelve likely lads became a captain. Garm had a gold collar, and while he lived roamed at his will, a proud and happy dog, insufferable to his fellows; for he expected all other dogs to accord him to respect due to the terror and splendour of his master. The grey mare passed to her days' end in peace and gave no hint of her reflections.

In the end Giles became a king, of course, the King of the Little Kingdom. He was crowned in Ham in the name of Ægidius Draconarius; but he was more often known as Old Giles Worming. For the vulgar tongue came into fashion at his court, and none of his speeches were in the Book-latin. His wife made a queen of great size and majesty, and she kept a tight hand on the household accounts. There was no getting round Queen Agatha – at least it was a long walk.

Thus Giles became at length old and venerable and had a white beard down to his knees, and a very respectable court (in which merit was often rewarded), and an entirely new order of knight-hood. These were the Wormwardens, and a dragon was their ensign: the twelve likely lads were the senior members.

It must be admitted that Giles owed his rise in a large measure to luck, though he showed some wits in the use of it. Both the luck and the wits remained with him to the end of his days, to the great benefit of his friends and his neighbours. He rewarded the parson very handsomely; and even the blacksmith and the miller had their bit. For Giles could afford to be generous. But after he became king he issued a strong law against unpleasant prophecy, and made milling a royal monopoly. The blacksmith changed to the trade of an undertaker; but the miller became an obsequious servant of the crown. The parson became a bishop, and set up his see in the church of Ham, which was suitably enlarged.

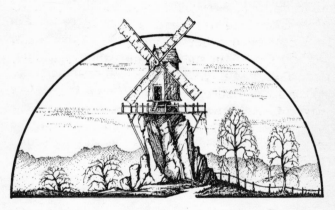

Now those who live still in the lands of the Little Kingdom will observe in this history the true explanation of the names that some of its towns and villages bear in our time. For the learned in such matters inform us that Ham, being made the chief town of the new realm, by a natural confusion between the Lord of Ham and the Lord of Tame became known by the latter name, which it retains to this day; for Thame with an *h* is a folly without warrant. Whereas in memory of the dragon, upon whom their fame and fortune were founded, the Draconarii built themselves a great house, four miles north-west of Tame, upon the spot where Giles and Chrysophylax first made acquaintance. That place became known throughout the kingdom as Aula Draconaria, or in the vulgar Worminghall, after the king's name and his standard.

The face of the land had changed since that time, and kingdoms have come and gone; woods have fallen, and rivers have shifted, and only the hills remain, and they are worn down by the rain and the wind. But still that name endures; though men now call it Wunnle (or so I am told); for villages have fallen from their pride. But in the days of which this tale speaks Worminghall it was, and a Royal Seat, and the dragon-standard flew above the trees; and all things went well there and merrily, while Tailbiter was above ground.

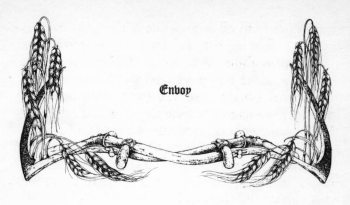

Envoy

Chrysophylax begged often for his liberty; and he proved expensive to feed, since he continued to grow, as dragons will, like trees, as long as there is life in them. So it came to pass, after some years, when Giles felt himself securely established, that he let the poor worm go back home. They parted with many expressions of mutual esteem, and a pact of non-aggression upon either side. In his bad heart of hearts the dragon felt as kindly disposed towards Giles as a dragon can feel towards anyone. After all there was Tailbiter: his life might easily have been taken, and all his hoard too. As it was, he still had a mort of treasure at home in his cave (as indeed Giles suspected).

He flew back to the mountains, slowly and laboriously, for his wings were clumsy with long disuse, and his size and his armour were greatly increased. Arriving home, he at once routed out a young dragon who had had the temerity to take

78

up residence in his cave while Chrysophylax was away. It is said that the noise of the battle was heard throughout Venedotia. When, with great satisfaction, he had devoured his defeated opponent, he felt better, and the scars of his humiliation were assuaged, and he slept for a long while. But at last, waking suddenly, he set off in search of that tallest and stupidest of the giants, who had started all the trouble one summer's night long before. He gave him a piece of his mind, and the poor fellow was very much crushed.

'A blunderbuss, was it?' said he, scratching his head. 'I thought it was horseflies!'

𝔉𝔦𝔫𝔦𝔰

or in the vulgar

THE END

For your free copy of

The Complete Tolkien Catalogue

please send a large stamped addressed envelope to:

The Sales Office Administrator
Trade Division
Unwin Hyman Ltd
15-17 Broadwick Street
LONDON
W1V 1FP

Books by J. R. R. Tolkien in Unwin Paperbacks

The Hobbit	£2.99 ☐
The Illustrated Hobbit	£8.95 ☐
The Lord of the Rings: one volume	£8.99 ☐
The Fellowship of the Ring	£3.99 ☐
The Two Towers	£3.99 ☐
The Return of the King	£3.99 ☐
The Silmarillion	£5.50 ☐
Unfinished Tales	£4.99 ☐
The Book of Lost Tales 1	£4.99 ☐
The Book of Lost Tales 2	£4.99 ☐
The Lays of Beleriand	£4.99 ☐
The Shaping of Middle-Earth	£4.99 ☐
The Lost Road	£4.99 ☐
The Return of the Shadow	£5.50 ☐
The Adventures of Tom Bombadil	£3.99 ☐
Farmer Giles of Ham	£3.99 ☐
Smith of Wootton Major	£3.99 ☐
Sir Gawain and the Green Knight	£2.95 ☐

Tolkien related books

The Complete Guide to Middle-Earth	£4.99 ☐
Journeys of Frodo	£6.99 ☐
J. R. R. Tolkien: a Biography	£5.99 ☐

All these books are available at your local bookshop or newsagent, or can be ordered direct by post. Just tick the titles you want and fill in the form below.

Name ....

Address ....

....

....

Write to Unwin Cash Sales, PO Box 11, Falmouth, Cornwall TR10 9EN

Please enclose remittance to the value of the cover price plus:

UK: 80p for the first book plus 20p for each additional book ordered to a maximum charge of £2.00.

BFPO: 80p for the first book and 20p for each additional book.

OVERSEAS INC. EIRE: £1.50 for the first book plus £1.00 for the second book and 30p for each additional book.

UNWIN HYMAN reserve the right to show new retail prices on covers, which may differ from those previously advertised in the text or elsewhere. Postage rates are also subject to revision.